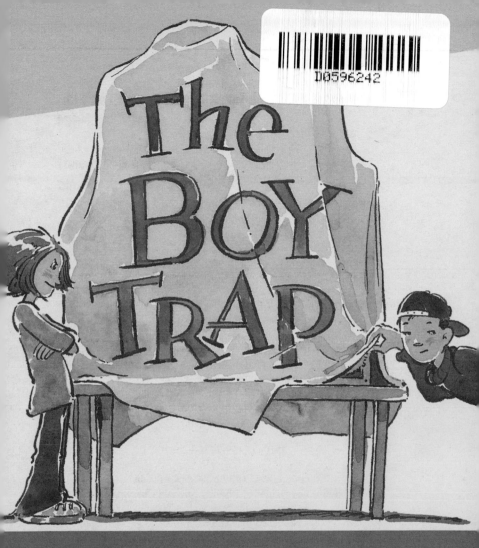

The BOY TRAP

by **Nancy Matson**

Pictures by **Michael Chesworth**

SCHOLASTIC INC.

New York Toronto London Auckland Sydney
Mexico City New Delhi Hong Kong

To Grandpa Venti, who loves books as much as I do.
—NM

To Girl Power!
—MC

ISBN 0-439-22365-2

Text copyright © 1999 by Nancy Matson
Illustrations copyright © 1999 by Michael Chesworth
All rights reserved.
Published by Scholastic Inc.
SCHOLASTIC and associated logos are trademarks and/or
registered trademarks of Scholastic Inc.

12 11 10 9 8 7 6 5 4   1 2 3 4 5 6/0

Printed in the U.S.A.   40

First Scholastic printing, January 2001

Designed by Anthony Jacobson

Chapter 1

● ●

Emma ran a quick hand through her hair as she watched Tommy, her neighbor, make figure eights with his new bike. She felt the brittle ends of each strand and frowned. Ever since her Aunt Marian had told Emma that her hair was her best feature, she brushed it frequently and was constantly monitoring its softness.

Tommy's movements flowed gracefully, and no one watching would suspect what a pig he was most of the time.

Forgetting her hair, Emma pushed up the sleeves of her white lab coat and, from her seated position on the sidewalk, tried to judge the forces that allowed Tommy to guide his bicycle with such accuracy. She was so consumed with the physics of what she was watching that her mind reduced the scene before her

$$a^2$$

$$t$$

$$b = 2wLr$$

$$r$$

$$\theta$$

$$2 \times 4 = 8$$

$$F = MA$$

$$C = 2\pi r$$

to a simple scientific problem. That was why, when Tommy screeched to a halt in front of her, spewing dirt and pebbles in her face, Emma was genuinely startled.

Tommy jumped off his bike, holding it by one handlebar, and looked Emma up and down. "Where'd you get that weird jacket?" he asked. "Why would you wear something so ugly?" He cracked his gum loudly and unclasped his hand, letting his bike crash to the ground.

Emma scooted over to avoid being scraped by his front tire. She gritted her teeth and tried to answer politely. "I'm going to be a scientist," she said, "and this jacket helps me think scientifically." Emma's aunt Marian, a chemical-engineering student at the University of Pennsylvania, had given her the jacket. When Emma grew up, she wanted to be as much like her aunt Marian as possible. But she certainly wasn't going to tell Tommy *that*.

"Well," said Tommy, "you can't know about science, because you're a girl, and girls don't know anything about that stuff. My dad's a biologist, but my mom hasn't been able to help me with my science homework since I was in fourth grade, because she doesn't know anything!"

As Tommy talked, Emma took a good hard look at him. Not only was he obnoxious, she decided, but ugly. Horribly ugly. His hair hung in his face like it wasn't hair at all but some substance that was half liquid and half solid. Every one of his expressions was sour. He looked as if he'd either just taken a swig of flat soda or been bitten by a small, annoying dog.

"Well, my aunt Marian is a scientist," Emma replied, though she didn't even want to mention her aunt's name to such a horrible boy. "And I'm going to be a scientist, too. Maybe your mom doesn't like science, but that doesn't prove anything."

Emma was proud of herself. She wasn't being insulting, like Tommy was. She was being factual. And that's what science is all about: facts.

Tommy picked up his bike and threw his leg over it. And just as Emma was feeling as though she'd accomplished something for the scientific community everywhere, Tommy screwed up his mouth, drew back, and spit his wad of gum right on her head.

Chapter 2

Tommy had ridden halfway down the block before
Emma recovered enough to stand up. "You stupid
jerk!" she yelled. She took a few steps toward him
and his bike, then stopped dead in her tracks. It was
bad enough that she should be standing there with
gum in her hair—she certainly didn't want to be seen
running down the street like a fool.

"I hate boys," Emma announced
a few minutes later, as her
mother attempted to remove
the gum from Emma's hair
with peanut butter and
sewing scissors. Emma
sat on a kitchen stool,
grimacing. "They're all
jerks!"

"I've known quite a few
nice boys in my time," her
mother said. "Your father was a
boy once, and you don't hate him."

"He must have grown out of it."

Emma's mother made a clicking
sound with her tongue as she sur-
veyed Emma's head. "Aren't you
kids a little old for this kind of
behavior?"

Emma was absolutely furious. "*I* didn't do anything!" she said. "I've never spit gum in anyone's hair in my whole life."

Mrs. Adams took a sharp breath of air. "Oh, Emma!" she said. "The scissors slipped, and I cut a little too much off." She stepped back a few feet to get a better view. "I don't think anyone will notice."

Then the phone rang, and Emma forgot about her hair. It was her best friend, Louise. Because she and Louise had been best friends for so long, their conversations didn't have beginnings or endings. Instead they'd had one four-year-long conversation.

"First of all," Louise said, "I'm in big trouble with my mom because I stayed after school to play basketball, and she needed me to wash vegetables. I told her she should've asked Eddie, but she said he was a terrible vegetable washer." Eddie was Louise's older brother. He was a real brain and never had to do any household chores. "Well, I told her that she may have needed someone to wash vegetables, but the kids needed someone, too. They needed someone to play basketball, and Eddie is a better vegetable washer than a basketball player. Since I couldn't do both things, Eddie should wash the vegetables.

"Well, she didn't think basketball was as important as food, so I told her that it was really important for me to play, because if I don't practice, I'll never make the junior-high team. Then I won't make the high-school team, and then I'll never get a scholarship for college, and she and Dad will have to fork out like a million dollars for my tuition or I'll end up working in a poultry factory, hacking the heads off chickens. I told her that if you're not really amazing by the end of the sixth grade, then you'll never make it. I told her I heard some coach on the radio say that.

"She didn't believe me, and now I have to wash and dry the dishes tonight for making up stories. Ugh."

It was tough to get a word in edgewise when Louise was telling one of her stories, but Emma usually found that the direct approach was the best. "Tommy spit gum in my hair."

"That kid's a moron," Louise replied instantly. One good thing about having a best friend, Emma thought, is that you can always count on her to take your side. "We're lucky his parents send him to private school."

"No girl would ever do that," Emma said. "Why do boys do such horrible things?"

"I don't know," said Louise.

"Boys are a waste of human life."

"Oh, Emma, come on. You can't base your whole theory about boys on one thing that happened. You're the one who told me that. It's called 'anecdotal evidence,' right? You said it wasn't very scientific."

"Yeah, I guess," said Emma. Louise was certainly no scientist, but she was right about that.

"Besides, I know you don't hate *all* boys," said Louise. Then she waited. Emma didn't say a word. She knew Louise was talking about Wally, the one boy in the whole fifth grade who might be O.K. Not definitely O.K., but just not definitely *not* O.K. All the other boys said obnoxious things, but Wally rarely even spoke. It wasn't much to go on, but Emma couldn't help hoping.

Emma never talked about Wally, so she wasn't sure how Louise knew what she thought of him. Sometimes, though, with your best friend, you don't have to say a word.

"So," asked Louise, after giving up on getting Emma to say something about Wally, "how was Roger today?" She'd asked Emma the same question every day after school since fifth grade started. Emma had what Louise regarded as the great fortune of being in the same class as Roger, the boy Louise currently liked. Emma, sadly, couldn't care less about getting to spend her whole day in Roger's presence.

Emma sighed. "He fell asleep during the Pledge of Allegiance and had to stay for detention. Plus, today Mrs. Marsh asked if anyone knew what *doomsday* meant, and Roger said it meant the first day of school."

Louise laughed and then became serious again. "I wonder why he's so tired. Maybe he was up late playing video games. Or maybe he's worried and can't sleep."

"Maybe boys just need sixteen hours of sleep a day, like cats," Emma suggested.

Louise grunted. "Well, I guess I better set the table. Eddie the Boy Wonder can't be expected to do it. He could be on the verge of discovering a cure for cancer or something."

After she hung up the phone, Emma examined her hair in the mirror and let out a high-pitched yelp. She had a bald spot right on top of her head. Why would her mother think no one would notice it? How could Tommy ruin her hair? It was her best feature! She'd have to wear a hat until it grew back. She'd be the only girl in school wearing a hat! She ran into her room, jumped into bed, and pulled the covers over her head.

Louise might be right about not basing all her opinions about boys on one incident, but that didn't prove Emma was *wrong* about boys. It just meant she should continue to gather evidence until she could *prove* boys were jerks. Emma grabbed a fresh notebook from the stack of blank ones under her bed. In block letters she wrote: BOY BOOK. On the first page she wrote: Tommy. *Spit gum on my hair for no reason.*

On the second page she wrote: Roger.

"**W**here'd you get that hat?" Roger asked Emma when he saw her in the hallway the next day. Emma was wearing her father's old fishing hat, which was the best head-covering she could find on short notice. Emma's dad had almost laughed out loud when she'd tried it on. He hadn't thought she'd noticed, but she had. She might be just a kid, but she wasn't blind!

Emma shrugged at Roger and kept walking. Why should he care where she got the hat? Why did boys always want to know where you got things?

She spotted Louise leaning against the wall. Her math book was open, and she was frantically adding up fractions. She was concentrating so hard she didn't even notice Roger.

Emma tapped her friend on the shoulder. "Why didn't you do that last night?" she asked.

"I'm terrible at math," Louise said. "It just makes me depressed." She slammed her book shut. "Besides, my mom decided that last night was the perfect time for me to get a head start on the spring cleaning."

"What about Eddie?"

"Please," said Louise. "He had to fix the garage-door opener. But for Eddie, that's like assigning him to eat candy bars while watching Saturday-morning cartoons."

Emma looked at the part of Louise's homework that was sticking out of her book. There were about a million cross-outs and eraser marks. Emma wished she could give her at least a few right answers to turn in, but she knew it wouldn't make any difference. What she really wanted to do was make Louise smarter.

Louise's notebook paper had bite marks on the upper corner. "Chewing on your homework?" asked Emma.

"Yeah, that's my new excuse," said Louise. "I ate my own homework." She rolled her eyes. "No, we've got mice. I saw one last night when I got up to get a glass of orange juice. Yuck!"

Emma made a disapproving face.

"My mom wants to kill them," Louise continued. "But I'm going to try to make one of those traps that catches them alive, and then I can just set them free in a field somewhere. I'm going to start tonight."

Chapter 3

Mrs. Marsh decided to begin the day with geography. Emma made a point of shooting a suspicious sidelong glance at each of the boys in the room, just so everyone knew where she stood on the topic of boys. She even included Wally, who might have been spared except that Emma didn't want to be considered a hypocrite.

"Who knows which country has the biggest population?" asked Mrs. Marsh.

Emma raised her hand. "China."

"That's right," Mrs. Marsh answered. Emma noticed her teacher's eyes glazing over slightly; she always got a little misty when she mentioned the Far East.

Wally caught Emma's eye and nodded at her significantly. Though he didn't speak much, he was quite a nodder. Emma felt an urge to smile at him but fought it, nodding back as neutrally as she could manage.

Roger, who was sitting next to Emma, leaned over and whispered, "How'd you know that?"

"Why are you so surprised?" Emma hissed back. "What do you think I am, stupid?" What was the matter with him? Why should she defend herself to him every minute? Emma took out her boy book and wrote on Roger's page: *Thinks girls don't know anything.*

At the end of the day, Emma searched the halls for Louise. They had plans to spend the afternoon at Emma's house, making collages out of magazine pictures. Finally she found her outside the cafeteria, talking to Wally. Even from a hundred feet away, she could tell by Louise's gestures that she was telling a complicated lie.

"So as far as I know, I have an actual rock from the Moon," Louise was saying as Emma came within earshot. "I mean, at least that's what I was told. I met the guy at a party my mother gave. He was an astronaut—not one of the famous ones, though. . . ."

Wally's eyes were wide with amazement. He barely looked at Emma as she joined them.

"Louise!" said Emma, figuring she should interrupt before her friend got herself in more trouble. "We should go." She didn't like the way Wally was looking at Louise. He never looked quite that interested when he was listening to *her*.

Once Louise started telling a story, stopping her was like chasing a rubber ball that was rolling downhill. "It's even a special kind of moon rock," Louise babbled. "There are only three others like it on Earth, and two are in the White House. . . ."

"Oh, Louise," said Emma, "are you telling that boring story about my uncle the astronaut again?"

Both Louise and Wally turned to stare at Emma. Emma was as surprised as they were. She wasn't supposed to be making up lies! But she sure had Wally's attention now.

Her face burning, Emma grabbed Louise by the arm. "C'mon, we have to go."

"I just couldn't stop myself," said Louise on their way out of the building. "I was talking to Wally and then I started thinking about how whatever I told him, he'd probably tell Roger. Then I got really nervous." She turned to Emma. "And what about you? Your uncle manages a movie theater."

Emma shrugged. "Yeah, I know."

Louise laughed. "You're supposed to be the scientific one."

"Well, I am," said Emma. She smiled, too. "At least mostly."

Emma knew this had just been a fluke. She never acted like that. Louise made up stories; Emma acted logically in every situation.

Suddenly Louise, who'd broken the Kennedy School record for the hundred-yard dash, tripped over her own shoelaces. That could only mean one thing: Roger.

Emma and Louise caught up with Roger and Wally as they all walked east on Main Street. It was obvious to Emma that the boys wanted them to catch up, and after Emma spotted them, she began walking as slowly as humanly possible.

"Hey, Emma," said Roger as she and Louise approached.

"Yeah?" asked Emma, bracing herself.

"You know what I like about Louise?" Roger asked in a stage whisper.

"What?" asked Emma.

Roger smiled right at Louise. "I like her crooked smile," he said.

Louise looked up at Roger and smiled.

"Crooked?" exclaimed Emma. "Her smile isn't crooked! It's perfectly fine!" She looked to Louise for support, but Louise kept on smiling as if she'd just been named Miss Pre-Teen America. Maybe her smile was a little bit crooked. But not so you'd really notice.

Roger waved, and Wally nodded, and they turned onto another street. It was just as well, Emma thought. Who knows what Louise might have said if they hadn't left?

"He can't even say something nice without turning it into an insult," said Emma.

"It's not an insult," said Louise. "Why do you have to take everything the wrong way?"

"Me? Take everything the wrong way? It's Roger's fault. He's such a jerk."

Louise stopped walking. "If you're going to act mean all afternoon, I'm going home. Are you?"

Emma *did* feel mean. She tried to think of something to say, but she couldn't come up with a single nice thing. She brimmed over with meanness. Louise stared at her, waiting, but Emma's lips wouldn't move.

"Fine. I'll see you tomorrow, then," Louise said, storming off in the direction of her own house.

Why was this happening? Emma wondered. She hated to fight with Louise. When you fight with your best friend, there's no one good to complain to about it.

Chapter 4

At school the next day, Mrs. Marsh opened her science book with a crack. "O.K., everybody," she said. "I want to talk to you about this year's science fair."

A mixed response rose from the class. Anna, who wanted to be a rocket scientist when she grew up, let out a low-grade cheer. Tony, who wanted to be a professional soccer player, made a disgusted grunt. Wally, Emma noticed, formed his lips into a secret smile.

"Since you're in the fifth grade now," said Mrs. Marsh, "you'll all be required to participate in the fair. If you have any questions about your project idea, you can ask me at the end of the day. The science fair will be held on May fifteenth."

"Also," she continued, "you'll have the opportunity again this year to enter the Young Inventors Contest. Please see me with any questions regarding that as well."

The Young Inventors Contest! Emma rolled her eyes. Entering that was, to most kids in school, the equivalent of standing up in the middle of the cafeteria and announcing that you were a complete loser. You might as well pee your pants during gym class, for all the points it got you.

But the science fair—now, that had possibilities.

At recess Emma spotted Louise sitting on a rock by the little kids' swingset, hunched over her note-

book. This was their usual meeting spot, so Emma took it as a good sign. Louise was sketching out some diagrams involving a series of pulleys and a milk crate.

"What are you doing?" asked Emma.

"I'm working on the mousetrap," Louise replied, without looking up. Her brow was furrowed.

"Yeah?" asked Emma. "Did you get Eddie to help?"

It was obvious from Louise's expression that Emma had said the wrong thing. Again. "That's what my mom asked me, too," said Louise in a quiet voice. "Nobody thinks I can do anything myself."

"That's not what I meant," said Emma. Then she sighed. *Was* that what she'd meant? She wasn't used to the idea of Louise being able to . . . well, to do anything hard by herself. But she didn't want Louise to feel bad. They were still best friends, as far as Emma knew. "Are we still in a fight?" Emma asked. "I'm sorry about yesterday. I was kind of a jerk."

"It's all right," said Louise. "Besides, how can I be in a fight with you? I might need help with my mousetrap, right?" Louise gave Emma one of her slightly crooked smiles. "But I do think you spend too much time thinking about every dumb thing every dumb boy says."

Emma thought about the boy notebook she had in her desk and was glad she hadn't mentioned it to Louise. She'd made another entry last night after their run-in with Roger and Wally. You can't tell even your best friend everything.

"Did you hear about the science fair?" Emma asked Louise.

"Yeah. I couldn't believe it," Louise said. "I thought we'd be fine until junior high. I don't know what I'm going to do. Why can't we ever get extra assignments in something I'm good at, like gym?"

"Don't worry, Louise," Emma told her. "All you need is a good idea. I'm sure you can think of one. My aunt Marian says everyone has good ideas." Emma wasn't at all sure that Louise could come up with something. But she certainly wasn't going to say that.

"Maybe I can just redo one of Eddie's old projects," Louise said.

Emma thought about what Eddie had done last year, rigging the school auditorium to create a mock solar eclipse. "Louise, they'll know. All the teachers love him. They probably keep a scrapbook of every homework assignment he's ever handed in. They'll remember."

"Yeah," said Louise. "I guess you're right."

Just then Emma spotted Wally. He nodded at her and Louise and hummed as he walked past. Emma recognized the tune as being from *West Side Story,* which her parents had on CD at home. Emma loved *West Side Story.* She took Wally's humming as a good sign. The next time she spoke to her aunt Marian, she'd have to ask her about signs.

When Emma returned to her desk after recess, she took out her notebook and turned to a fresh page. At the top she wrote: Wally. *I like him. No reason.* Then she closed the notebook and shoved it under her science book.

The bell rang, and Mrs. Marsh stood up. "By the way," she said, "for your science project you may work with a partner. However, this does not mean you only have to do half as much work. I expect group projects to be more comprehensive."

Emma turned around in her chair to look at Wally. They would be perfect partners! They were both good students and loved science. It wasn't personal. It just made sense. Anyone could see that.

"For those of you who would prefer to work in teams, I'd like you to let me know by the end of the day tomorrow."

Emma gave Wally a nod, and Wally nodded back, confirming that he agreed! It was all settled. She'd call him that night to make the final arrangements.

Maybe Louise was right. Maybe Emma was too

hard on boys. But maybe being partners with Wally would change things. Now she could see if Wally really was the one nice boy in the fifth grade.

Chapter 5

Emma had two phone calls to make. The first was to Aunt Marian.

"I always loved the science fair," said Aunt Marian. "I was a nerd even as a child."

Emma unraveled the telephone cord with one hand and felt the top of her head with the other, checking to see if her bald spot had grown in over the last week. It hadn't.

"I don't know what to pick for my topic," said Emma. "I want it to be something really good."

"Well, the important thing is that you choose something you're interested in," Aunt Marian told her. "If you pick something that just sounds good, you'll regret it later."

Emma was reminded of a bread-mold project she'd seen at last year's fair. Who wanted to spend three months studying bread mold?

"You also want to think of something original," Aunt Marian added. "A lot of projects are big yawns. Like those solar ovens—boring. Or they're really general and don't prove anything, like when some kid just gets out a bunch of plastic dinosaur models and talks about which one's a herbivore and which one's a carnivore. Who cares, you know? A real science project has a hypothesis, something you're trying to prove. It shouldn't be just a rehash of obvious facts."

Emma felt stumped. "This is going to be harder than I thought," she said.

"It won't be, Emma, because everything interests you. Just pick something and try to think of a new angle on it. Think of something that might be true, and then do some research and prove that it *is* true. It's fun to back up your ideas with facts. That's the power of science."

"Well," said Emma, "I'll think about it." She paused for a second before she asked her next question. "Aunt Marian?"

"Uh-huh?"

"Do you believe in signs?"

Aunt Marian let out a little laugh. "You mean signs as in omens?"

"Yeah."

"That's just superstitious. It's got nothing to do with science, you know."

Emma could tell Aunt Marian was teasing her a

little bit. "Yeah, I know."

"Well," Aunt Marian said, "sometimes I get a little superstitious, too. I just tell myself that I'm picking up on things science has yet to explain."

Emma liked that answer. "I think I'm picking up on things like that, too."

For Emma's second call, she had to consult her local phone book. Her parents sat down on either side of her at the kitchen table just as she found Wally's number.

"So, Emma," said Mr. Adams, "how's that hat working out for you?"

Emma gave her hat a tug. She shrugged. "O.K."

"What's all this your mother tells me about you hating boys?"

Emma looked over at her mother but could make nothing of her expression. "I don't hate them," said Emma, trying to remain calm. "I just don't . . . appreciate their company." There! thought Emma. That was reasonable, wasn't it?

Mr. Adams laughed.

"Emma," said Mrs. Adams, "we're just worried about you. It's O.K. if you don't like boys right now, but sometimes you can come off as a little hostile. First the fight with Tommy and now with Louise."

How did her mother know about the fight with Louise? Probably from Louise's mom. But Emma refused to ask about it. She didn't want the conversation to last any longer than it had to.

She looked at her father. He didn't seem the least bit worried about her. He probably wouldn't worry no matter what she did. It was just what she'd expect from a former boy.

"Between you and Louise," said Mrs. Adams. "Honestly. You hating boys and her being boy crazy."

"She's not boy crazy," said Emma. "And I told you, I don't hate boys. I was right about to call one." She wasn't going to get mad. She wasn't ill-tempered, like some people.

"Well, in that case," said Mr. Adams to Emma's mother, "shall we?" They left the kitchen arm in arm, making a big show of it. Honestly, thought Emma.

She wished her parents had had more kids. Then maybe they'd have someone else to pester once in a while.

The phone at Wally's house was picked up after one ring. "Hello, hello, and hello," answered a man's voice. Emma figured it had to be Wally's father.

"Hello," said Emma, "could I speak to Wally, please?"

"Wally?" the man said. "Yes, I believe there's a Wally here. I'll see if he's available."

People's parents could be a real pain sometimes, Emma thought. They felt like they could say anything they wanted to you, just because you were a kid. They were forever referring to girls as "young ladies." Emma could tell from the way Wally's dad had spoken to her that he was telling Wally there was a "young lady" on the line for him.

"Hello," said Wally tentatively. Emma didn't even recognize his voice, since she hardly ever heard it. It was a nice voice.

"Hi, Wally. This is Emma." She took a deep breath. "I was just calling to talk about the science fair."

"The science fair?" asked Wally. Then he was silent.

Well, thought Emma, I should have expected to be in charge of this conversation. "If we're going to be partners, we should figure out what our topic will be so we can tell Mrs. Marsh. You still want to be partners, don't you?"

Silence. Emma was starting to realize that, when you're talking to someone who communicates largely by nodding, face-to-face conversations are probably a lot more efficient than using the phone.

"I . . ." Wally said. "I'm going to be partners with Roger."

"Roger?" Emma felt incredibly stupid. Though Wally's comment was quite simple, she seemed unable to process it. He had never actually said he wanted to be partners with Emma. Why had she thought it was so obvious? "O.K.," she said. "Bye." Then she slammed down the phone so Wally didn't have a chance to reply.

She reached for her notebook and uncapped her favorite blue pen. On the Wally page she wrote: *Just like all other boys.*

That's when she got her idea for the science fair.

Chapter 6

"Eddie Zarotsky is your brother?" Roger was asking Louise as Emma approached them. They were leaning against the front of the school, killing time before the first bell rang. Emma recognized this as the start of yet another conversation about what a genius Eddie was. He was a legend throughout Kennedy Elementary.

"Yeah," Louise admitted. "Technically."

"Wow," said Roger. "I heard he doesn't have to do homework because he already knows everything."

Emma heard Louise sigh. "Actually he's one of those, uh, savants? I forget what you call them. He's really good at school, but he can't do anything else. Every time he makes a phone call, I have to dial it for him."

Emma felt like she should take some preventive measure and step in before Louise's story got out of hand. "Hey, you guys," she said, smiling at both of them. Since she'd come up with her idea for the science fair, she was in a friendly mood, even toward Roger.

"You're lucky you come from such a smart family," Roger said to Louise, "because then you know you're probably pretty smart, too."

Louise positively glowed. A part of Emma was glad to see her friend so happy, though the other part of her wanted to throw up. Then the bell rang, and Roger took his cue to exit. Happily, Emma was spared any further sappy conversation.

Louise and Emma walked side by side down the hall. "He thinks I'm smart," said Louise. She took a long time between steps as she walked, as if she were using her legs for the first time. "I never thought it could be good to have Eddie as a brother."

Emma shrugged noncommittally. "Listen, Louise, I want to talk to you after school about the science fair."

Louise snapped back to reality. "I tried to look through Eddie's books last night to get some ideas, but he freaked when he saw me. I don't know what to do."

"Come over after school, and we'll figure it out. I've got an idea."

As soon as Emma sat down at her desk, Wally was beside her. He looked extremely concerned.

"Emma, I'd already promised Roger . . ."

"It's all right," Emma answered casually. Only yesterday she would've been happy to have Wally come over and speak to her. Now it no longer mattered. *He* no longer mattered. "Forget it," she told him.

Wally, having used up his allotted words for the day, trudged back to his desk, defeated. Emma pulled down on her hat and waited for the school day to end.

Chapter 7

Emma wrote out several mathematical formulas: $(B + G) * 3 = +/- 17x + 6y$. Then she drew a few sets of bar graphs on sheets of paper she'd posted on her bedroom wall. Louise, licking chocolate frosting off a spoon, sat on Emma's bed and watched. Emma glanced at the bed's horrible, frilly white canopy. She was always reminded of how much she hated her bed when someone else sat on it.

$(B+G)$
$*3 = +/. 17x$
$+ 6y$

"That's algebra," complained Louise as Emma made her notes. "You don't know algebra. Even Eddie only knows a little."

Emma made a sweeping gesture. "Forget about all these charts for a minute," she said, putting her red marker in the pocket of her white lab coat. "I just want to outline what I'm trying to do here. I've been collecting evidence for a few weeks now, and for my science project, I want to prove that girls are better than boys."

"*Prove* that girls are better?" Louise was at complete attention. "Can you do that?"

Emma smiled. "Sure. You can prove anything that's true. That's what science is for."

"But," said Louise, "is it really true?"

"You know it's true, don't you? Maybe every boy's not so terrible, but aren't all the girls you know smarter and nicer and more interesting than the boys?"

Louise scrunched up her forehead. "Well, maybe . . ."

"It's true, Louise. I'm telling you. And I think we can prove it."

"We?" asked Louise.

"You've got to be my partner. It'll be the best project from Kennedy Elementary since Eddie graduated."

Louise jumped up from the bed. "I'll do it. But now I better get home before my mom starts screaming her head off." She got a faraway look. "Wouldn't it be great if we won? I've never even gotten a B in science before!"

After Louise left, Emma reviewed her wall charts and wrote out a few more notes. Then she took off her hat and inspected her bald spot with her fingers. She was pretty sure she could feel a few hairs growing in.

Chapter 8

●●

"**O**.K.," said Emma, handing Louise a clipboard and pen, "here's what we're going to do today." The two girls huddled outside Kennedy Elementary, next to the lone tree that marked the school's front lawn. Curious eyes watched them from all sides. Ever since they'd announced their topic for the science fair, Emma and Louise had been the subject of not only curiosity, but supportive back slaps, disapproving glances, thumbs up, thumbs down, anonymous and signed notes (both pro and con), and numerous offers of assistance. All of these reactions were divided along gender lines.

Emma had heard a variety of stories first-, second-, and even third-hand about the impact of their project. A third-grade girl had punched a third-grade boy in the jaw after he publicly mocked the idea that girls were superior to boys. Emma had personally witnessed a bunch of boys in the playground, representing all six grades, drawing sloppy pictures of Louise and Emma in chalk on the ground, then throwing rocks at them. This frightened Emma slightly, but mostly she was upset that they drew her with such an unbelievably large chin.

Emma felt she'd been taking the attention pretty well, but she was worried about Louise. Louise had barely spoken about any of the controversy surrounding the project, but Emma had caught her defending them with involved lies ("Girls actually use more of their brains than boys, for one thing. . . ."), and Emma was worried that she was ruining their credibility. She'd also noticed that Roger had avoided Louise since the announcement. Though Emma felt this was for the best, she knew Louise wasn't happy about it.

Emma knew it didn't matter what anybody said. This was about science, not opinion. She tapped a pen against her clipboard. "Today we're going to test for politeness."

"I thought we were testing for strong character," said Louise. "Bravery, honesty, stuff like that. Who cares about politeness?"

"I know," said Emma, "but we can't just wait around until some kid does something brave. That could take days."

"I guess," said Louise. "But still."

"It's important to be civilized, right? And being polite shows you're civilized."

"All right," said Louise. "Let's try it."

"Every time a boy or girl uses a polite word, make a checkmark in this column, and every time they say something rude, make a checkmark over here. I'll do the same thing in my class. At the end of the day, we'll compare."

Emma tried to give Louise what she thought was an encouraging nod and a smile. Louise didn't notice. She was too busy looking nervously around as if she were some little kid on the first day of school.

Once the bell rang, Emma sat down at her desk with a sense of purpose. She uncapped her pen so forcefully that the cap flew under the desk next to her.

"Could you please give me that pen cap?" she asked Jeff Harrington, who sat next to her. Her hand went automatically to make a check in the Girls/Polite column until she realized it probably wouldn't be right to include herself in her own survey. Jeff gave her an icy look, scooped up the pen cap, and handed it over.

"Could I please go to the girls' room?" asked Robin, halfway into history class. Mrs. Marsh nodded, and Emma made her first check under the category Girls/Polite.

"Could I go to the boys' room?" asked Mark. "Please?" he added as an afterthought. Emma didn't feel this *please* was as heartfelt as Robin's, but she duly recorded a check under Boys/Polite.

And so it went throughout the day. Emma made checkmarks and notes on her clipboard. Some kids looked at Emma with interest, but none of them asked her what she was doing.

After lunch Emma noticed Jeff studying her clipboard. She clasped her notes to her chest, but it was too late. Jeff whispered to Roger, and Roger smiled for the first time in

days. Soon they were whispering and passing notes to every boy in the room.

"Does anyone know which kind of blood cells carry oxygen?" asked Mrs. Marsh. Every boy in the class shot his hand in the air. Mrs. Marsh lifted one eyebrow. "Brian?"

"Thanks for calling on me, Mrs. Marsh," said Brian, from the third row. He looked over at Emma. Emma winced and put a check down on her clipboard. "Could you please repeat the question, because I forgot it. Thanks a lot." Brian gave Emma an angelic smile, and Emma recorded checkmarks, pressing harder on her pen than she needed to.

"Which blood cells carry oxygen, Brian?"

"Thank you very much for repeating the question. I'm sorry to say I don't know the answer. I'm really sorry."

"Roger?" asked Mrs. Marsh. "Do you know the answer?"

"I do, Mrs. Marsh. Thank you for calling on me." Emma could barely write fast enough to keep up. "Please give me just a second." Roger looked thoughtful. "Thanks for waiting. I think the answer is *red* blood cells, right?"

"That's correct, Roger."

"Well, thank you for letting me answer."

This sort of excessive politeness went on for the rest of the afternoon until Emma gave up and stopped making checkmarks at all. It was maddening. Mrs. Marsh seemed eager for the day to be over as well. Emma spent the last forty-five minutes of class writing on the Roger page of her boy notebook as she hid behind her social studies textbook.

After school Emma unlocked the door of her house and made a beeline for the phone to call Louise. She didn't even take off her coat.

"The boys ruined the experiment," she told Louise without even saying hello. "They figured out what I was doing and then they just kept saying 'please' and 'thank you' in every sentence. My results are no good."

"That's terrible," said Louise. "We can still use mine, though. I just made all my checkmarks in the columns of my notebook so everyone would think I was taking notes. I'm copying the marks onto the clipboard now."

"I guess that's what I should've done," said Emma. How could Louise have thought of that and not her? "Maybe you should come over, and we could count up the checkmarks and decide what it means."

"I can't today, Emma. My mom keeps bugging me about getting rid of those mice. She also told me I had to clip the front hedges. I have to get started before it gets dark."

"Why can't Eddie clip the hedges?" asked Emma.

"I asked my mom, but she said last time he did it, she hardly had any hedges left."

Emma shook her head. Poor Louise. "How's the mousetrap going?" She couldn't help thinking Louise was wasting her time. Not everyone could invent things. It took a certain type of person—a scientific type.

"I think I've got all the parts I need, and I'm going to set it up tonight. I could really use some help from Eddie now that I have to put it together, but my mother warned me not to bother him because he's working on *his* science project. Not that she cares about *my* project. I told her I was doing one, but I'm not even sure she was listening."

"That's so unfair!" said Emma. "It's just because he's a boy and you're not. That doesn't mean your project isn't just as important."

"Nothing I could do would be as important as what he's doing," said Louise. "I am getting pretty tired of having to do all the work around here, though."

It just wasn't fair. Slavery was supposed to have ended over a hundred years ago, and here was Louise's mother trying to bring it back single-handed.

"Well, things'll be different after our science project is done," Emma reminded her friend. "If we can just prove that girls are superior, she'll at least have to make Eddie wash the dishes."

"I don't know, Emma. I think it's going to take a lot more than a fifth-grade science project," said Louise. "She probably wouldn't even ask him to take out the trash unless some new law was passed." She sighed. "I'll count up the marks tonight and let you know what I get tomorrow."

After she hung up, Emma wandered into the bathroom to do her daily head check. The bald spot was still there. And she was beginning to hate her father's floppy, army green hat. On the way back to her room, she passed her mother in the hallway.

"How's Louise doing?" asked Mrs. Adams.

"She's O.K.," said Emma, edging past her.

"Her mother and I had lunch today," said Mrs. Adams.

Figures, thought Emma. Mothers are always having lunch together.

"She was bragging about how helpful Louise is around the house, even building a trap for the mice. I thought you were the big scientist—I don't see you building anything to help me." Mrs. Adams smiled at Emma, but Emma wasn't buying it. "I thought you told me Louise doesn't get very good grades," continued Mrs. Adams. "So how come she's so smart at home?"

"I think her grades are about to improve, if you want to know the truth." With that, Emma made her escape, slamming her bedroom door behind her. She lay down on her bed and leafed through her boy notebook, looking for clues into the minds of boys. Then, in frustration, she turned to the Wally page and wrote about a hundred question marks.

Chapter 9

The next day, Emma stood in front of Mrs. Marsh's desk with her arms crossed. It was during recess, so she and Mrs. Marsh were the only people in the room.

"Emma, I can't give you everyone's grades," said Mrs. Marsh. "That wouldn't be ethical. And you're the second student today who's made that request."

Emma's mind paused on the second-student part, then immediately returned to her original question. "You don't have to tell me the names that go with the grades. Couldn't I just get a list of all the boys' grades and then all the girls'? It would really help my project. Please, Mrs. Marsh?"

Emma rarely used words like *please* and *thank you,* because they seemed unnecessary. But since the politeness survey, she was trying to work them in more. She didn't want to bring down the cause.

"Well, Emma, I guess I could do that. But it will take me a few days. And the grades won't be available for just you—they'll be open to the entire class."

"Great!" Emma said. "Thanks a lot." She didn't care if the entire world got copies. She was the only one who could do anything with the information— she and Louise, of course.

Emma ran into Wally on her way back to the schoolyard. After giving Emma a polite nod, he disappeared into Mrs. Marsh's room. Something clicked in Emma's head—it was then that she realized who the other person asking for the grades was.

"**W**hy would Wally want everyone's grades?" Emma asked Louise as they hunched over a table in the cafeteria, reviewing their politeness data.

"Who knows, with that kid." Louise leaned back in her chair and put her finger between her teeth, chewing on it for a moment. "Unless he's just trying to fake us out."

"Fake us out?" asked Emma.

"Yeah," said Louise. Emma could tell by Louise's intense expression that she was really warming up to the idea. "You know, the boys can't be too happy about our project. Maybe they're just going to start doing things to make us nervous so we'll spend all our time trying to figure out what they're doing instead of working on our project."

"Maybe," said Emma. She hadn't thought about that. Maybe she should concentrate more. She scanned the room for suspicious activity. "What are those two doing over there?" Emma pointed her fork at Wally and Roger, who were huddled together, reviewing documents of some kind.

Louise looked over at them—well, at least at Roger—and shrugged. "Probably working on their science project. That's all anybody's doing."

It was true. Ever since the announcement of Louise and Emma's project, the whole fifth grade seemed to throw themselves into the assignment with renewed interest. A quick scan of the room revealed at least fifteen kids, alone or with a partner, looking more interested in their notes and library books than in their lunches. Aunt Marian would be proud.

"You're probably right," said Emma. "But there's something about it I just don't like." She stared at the totals from yesterday, tapping her pencil against the piece of paper. *Boys: 40 polite words, Girls: 34.* "And this isn't good, either."

"But the boys talked a lot more," Louise was quick to point out. "Maybe we can do some kind of percentage thing."

She made a face after she said that, realizing, as Emma knew, that neither of them had any idea how to do that kind of complex calculation.

"The boys also made way more rude comments," Louise noted. She sighed. "But, like I said, they talked more. I don't really know if any of this proves anything."

Emma became suddenly aware that an intricate note-passing was going on. Some fourth-grade girl behind Wally and Roger wrote something on a slip of paper and folded it into a football shape. She chucked it to a girl who stood by the tray stack. That girl then dropped it in the lap of the girl next to her, who slid it, with one flick of the wrist, down four tables connected lengthwise. The note stopped in front of a first-grader, who picked it up and walked it over to Emma.

Emma and Louise looked at each other and then at the note. Emma quickly unfolded it.

It read, "Wally and Roger are working on something that looks like your project. At the top of the paper it says, 'Boys vs. Girls: Politeness.'" Then, in bold letters, "**BE CAREFUL.**"

Emma looked over at the note writer, who shook her head to indicate her disapproval.

But what was going on? "Why would they be doing the same thing we are?" said Emma. "It doesn't make sense."

"Emma," said Louise, "don't you get it? They're doing our project, but the other way. They're trying to prove boys are better than girls."

Emma clamped her mouth to prevent herself from making a loud animal sound. She didn't want Wally or Roger to see her upset. She felt a wave of panic, then a wave of embarrassment. How come Louise knew right away what was happening while she was still figuring it out? Emma was in charge of the project—not officially, of course, but she was obviously the smarter science partner.

Even that fourth-grader knew what was happening. That's why she'd written **BE CAREFUL.**

Louise's face crumpled. "If they're doing that, then Roger must just hate me. That's why he hasn't been very nice to me lately."

"Oh, Louise," Emma said, putting her hand on her friend's arm, "he doesn't hate you. It isn't personal, you know? It's just a science project."

"It's not just a science project, and you know it," said Louise, refusing to be comforted. "The only boy I ever really liked, and I made him hate me." She slammed her notebook shut. "And he thought I was smart."

The bell rang for fifth period, and Emma filed out of the cafeteria, Louise trailing behind her. A sixth-grade boy stuck out his arm to stop Emma from passing. He reached forward to flick at her head.

"Nice hat," he said sarcastically. "It makes you look like Gilligan."

Emma put her hand on her head to make sure the hat hadn't come off. Gilligan? From *Gilligan's Island*? Did she really look like him? She wished her hair had grown in and the science fair was over and she was finally in college and away from all this! She ducked under the boy's arm and ran.

Chapter 10

● ●

The next day at recess, Emma kept a watchful eye on Wally and Roger. They were surrounded by about thirty kids in the far corner of the playground. Roger took a piece of paper off the top of a stack of white, lined sheets and stood in front of the group. He folded it into an airplane and tossed it into the wind. The kids looked on.

Wally then removed a clipboard from under his arm and made notes. Roger produced a tape measure and called out the flight distance. Emma watched, horrified, as Wally wrote it down.

She stomped over to Wally and began talking before he even looked up. "This is for your science project? Who cares who makes better paper airplanes?" Even though Wally was a boy, Emma had expected a little better from him as far as science went. "I'm glad we didn't get to be partners, if this is what you're doing!" she said, sounding more hostile than she'd meant to.

Wally's eyes flickered as if they were suddenly changing color. "Are you doing your project because of me? I . . ."

Because of him! Boys always thought everything was about them. Emma was interested in her topic only for the sake of science.

But why did she suddenly feel so terrified?

"It has nothing to do with that," said Emma.

"What do you mean, who cares who makes better paper airplanes?" Roger interrupted. "It's hard to make a good paper airplane. The nose has to be the right shape so it doesn't instantly fall to the ground, and the wings have to be big enough to make it go really fast. A kid who can make a good paper airplane shows potential to do a lot of important work later on." He glared at Emma. "A kid who can make a good paper airplane is a lot better off than some kid who just says 'please' a lot, if you ask me."

For the first time since the gum incident, Emma was glad to be wearing her hat. With the way her face was burning, she would've been happy to have been wearing a ski mask.

How could Louise like anyone who was so impossible?

"At least I'm not a thief, like you!" Emma said to Roger. "At least I think of my own ideas for science projects!"

Then she whirled to face Wally. "And you, I thought you were different!"

Emma bit her lip after she said that. She hadn't wanted to let on that she thought of Wally as being different from any other boy—especially now that it was obvious he wasn't.

"You'd do the same thing," Wally spat out. "We have to."

"Yeah, Emma," said Roger. "If we'd decided to prove that boys were better than girls first, you would have tried to prove we were wrong. You would've had to do it and you know it."

Several more boys joined Wally and Roger, all staring at Emma.

"What makes you think you're better than us?" one yelled.

"Yeah," said another boy. "What's your problem?"

Emma backed away, scanning the growing group. She could see only one pair of friendly eyes: Wally's. They seemed to be saying how sorry he was about the whole thing.

Emma knew it didn't make sense, but she was starting to feel really scared. She didn't want to look like a coward, but she just had to get out of there. She turned on her heels and ran.

On her way into the building, she was hit from behind by a dozen paper airplanes. All of them were made by boys.

Chapter 11

"**I**'ve got some good news and some bad news," Louise told Emma several days later at their daily pre-homeroom meeting under the tree. "Which do you want first?"

Just then, a boy in the fourth grade walked purposefully up to Emma but said nothing. He waited for about thirty seconds, then walked away.

Emma stared after him. "What's that all about?" she asked Louise.

"That's the first piece of news. I'm pretty sure all the boys have made a pact not to talk to us."

"Just us two?" asked Emma.

"No, I mean all the girls."

Something clicked with Emma. As a rule, she didn't usually have a lot of conversations with boys, but in the last forty-eight hours she hadn't so much as heard a rude comment from one of them. Unconsciously, she'd known there was something going on, but she hadn't really gotten it until just then.

"Yeah," said Emma, "I guess I knew that."

"Roger hasn't said anything to me in two days," said Louise. "He hasn't been very friendly since this project was announced, but now he walks by me and makes a point of saying nothing. It's the same with the other boys—Wally used to talk to me sometimes, and now he acts like he's afraid of me."

As soon as Wally's name was mentioned, Emma had an incredible urge to change the subject. She didn't like even hearing Louise mention his name, let alone how friendly they used to be. It bugged her, though she couldn't say why.

"I guess that's the bad news, right?" Emma asked.

Louise snapped at her. "Of course that's the bad news. Don't you even care that half the world is mad at you?"

"Well, I don't think every boy in Australia is mad at us."

"They will be when they find out what we're doing."

Emma knew Louise wasn't worried about half the world being mad at her—she didn't even know half the world. She was just worried about Roger.

A bunch of second-grade boys stood nearby, crossing their arms and aggressively chewing their gum in Louise and Emma's direction. The last thing Emma wanted was to have a bunch of boys see her and Louise having a fight. They'd enjoy it way too much.

"But, Louise," said Emma, shooting the second-graders a look that moved them back a few paces, "they shouldn't be mad at us. We're not doing anything wrong. Even if you're trying to prove something that's unpopular, it's O.K. to do it if it's true." Aunt Marian had warned her that science could be controversial.

"Well, we should remember that if it turns out not to be true, we have to admit it," said Louise.

Emma knew there was no way that could happen. Of course, if in some future experiment on some other topic she turned out to be wrong, she would definitely admit it. "Right," said Emma. "Sure we would."

Emma saw that the second-grade boys had lost interest and were now pulling up wads of grass and throwing them at each other.

"What's the good news?" Emma wanted to know. She sure needed some.

Louise perked up immediately. "I finished the mousetrap, and it works! I caught a mouse! You've got to come over later and see it!"

"Wow," said Emma. "I'll come over after school." She couldn't help but wonder if Louise had gotten some help from Eddie in the end, but she knew it wouldn't be a good idea to ask. Anyway, even if Louise had only done part of the work, it was still really amazing that her mousetrap worked.

The second-graders had come back with a sign, which they were now holding up. Signs, it seemed, were O.K., just no actual talking. The sign was directed toward Emma and read, "Hey, Gilligan, NICE HAT!"

Emma's face felt hotter and hotter as Louise dragged her by the arm into school.

That night Emma began a new section in her boy book, entitled General Comments. She wrote: *Boys are stupid even when they don't talk. If I had been born a boy, I would be too embarrassed to leave my house.*

Chapter 12

●●●●●●●●●●●●●●●●●●●●●●●●●●●●●●●●●●●●●●

"**Y**ou have to remember," Emma's aunt Marian was telling her over the phone, "if you twist your data around, you can prove practically anything. When someone makes up a hypothesis, it's usually because they really believe something's true. Sometimes, because of that, people's experimentation methods aren't objective."

Sometimes Emma felt like her aunt Marian forgot she was only in the fifth grade. She both liked and disliked that about her. "What do you mean?" Emma asked.

"I mean, their research seems to support their hypothesis, but the research itself isn't conducted in a fair way. Even though you read a scientific report, and all the facts make it seem like something is being proved, sometimes it's just because the researchers picked only the facts that prove what they want to prove, and they left out things that might prove the opposite."

Emma was indignant. "What's the point of science if you're not going to be fair about something?"

"Well, Emma, you're right. The trouble is, sometimes people conduct invalid experiments by accident. Because they can't see how their own prejudices are clouding their work."

Suddenly Emma felt panicky. What if *she* did that? That would be awful. It was important for her to be fair now so she knew that she'd be fair when she was older and a real scientist. "How do you know if you're being fair?"

Aunt Marian sighed. "There's not an easy way to tell. You should just make sure your experiments get all sides of the story. And you've got to examine your own feelings about your subject and find out if they're affecting your research." She laughed a little. "I mean, if it's something that you can really have an opinion on. I'm doing some garlic research right now and, believe me, I have no prejudices about the scientific properties of garlic."

Emma bit her lip. It seemed like every time she talked to Aunt Marian, she had to practically rethink her entire life. She tugged at her hat. "Aunt Marian, the kids at school call me Gilligan. Because of my hat. But I have to wear it until my hair comes back in."

"H'm." Aunt Marian always took Emma's problems seriously. "Your mother mentioned you weren't too happy about wearing that hat." Emma had told her aunt about the gum incident, of course, but she tended to forget that Aunt Marian also got information from her mother. They were sisters, after all.

"Have you seen any more signs lately?" Aunt Marian asked.

"Sometimes," said Emma. "I watch for them. A black cat crossed my path, but it was really old and not very scary, so I'm pretty sure it didn't mean anything."

"Well, maybe sometime soon. What's your favorite color?"

"Green," Emma replied.

Two days later, by overnight mail, Emma received a package containing a green felt hat with a black band. It fit her exactly.

She took it as a sign.

Chapter 13

Louise sighed at Emma and looked at the baby-blue sky, distracted. They were standing by the tree before school.

"What'd you figure out?" Emma asked. They'd both gotten the class grades from Mrs. Marsh's room and had taken them home to analyze them separately. Today they were supposed to compare their results.

"Oh, I don't know," Louise said. "They seem about the same, I guess." She kicked one of her sneakers with the other one. "It's a good thing we aren't using my class, because my bad grades would ruin it for the girls for sure."

"Louise!" Emma said loudly. She couldn't stand to see her friend so down on herself. "You're really smart." After she'd said it, she realized it was true. "I know your grades aren't great, but grades don't always prove anything."

"If they don't prove anything," said Louise, "then why are we using them for one of our experiments?" She looked as if she might cry, and if she cried, Emma wouldn't be able to stand it.

"I don't know," said Emma weakly.

"If Roger doesn't ever talk to me again," Louise said suddenly, "I don't know how I'm going to make it through the fifth grade."

Emma knew that's what her friend was really upset about, even though it seemed like it had nothing to do with their conversation. The good thing about having a best friend is that you know the other person will understand, even if you don't explain everything.

As Emma was trying to think of something to say to make Louise feel better, she noticed a figure behind the nearby tree. It was Tommy, the gum-spitter. Emma instinctively touched her bald spot through her green felt hat.

"So you think girls are better than boys, huh?" Tommy yelled. He came tearing out from behind the tree and ran right up to Emma, then grabbed her hat and kept running.

"Hey!" shouted Emma. "Give me back my hat!" It was a waste of breath. Tommy obviously knew she wanted the hat back. She threw down her books and started running after him, covering her bald spot with her hand.

Louise, fast on her feet even when depressed, bolted in front of Emma, almost overtaking Tommy. Then, abruptly, she stopped. Emma followed Louise's glance and noticed a movement behind an old oak tree up ahead.

As Tommy advanced, Wally stepped from behind the tree and stuck his foot out, right in Tommy's path.

What was the matter with boys that they liked to spend so much time standing behind trees?

Tommy fell hard onto the ground, skidding for several feet. Emma could tell he was suppressing an urge to cry out in pain. The hat, which had flown out of his hand when he fell, landed by the oak. Wally picked it up and brought it over to Emma.

She grabbed it and pulled it over her head. "Thanks, Wally. Thanks a lot." Wally only nodded and then headed for school. Emma couldn't help wondering if he hadn't spoken because of the talking ban or if it was just his natural quietness.

Louise tapped Emma on the shoulder and handed her the books she'd dropped. "I guess maybe private schools have the day off today," she said, indicating Tommy.

"I guess so," said Emma. Then she ran to catch up with Wally. "I know you can't talk to me," she said, wanting to talk to him more than she'd wanted to talk to anyone in a long time. She reached into her pocket for a piece of paper and a pen and awkwardly shoved them toward Wally. "But maybe you could write something."

Wally wrote "Sorry" in block letters on the page.

"Sorry for what?" asked Emma. "You just got my hat back."

"Sorry," he wrote, "that you hate boys because of me."

"Hate boys?" Emma asked, perplexed. "But I . . ."

Out of the corners of their eyes, both Emma and Wally could see Roger approaching from far away. Without exchanging any more information, written or spoken, they faced away from each other and slowly drifted apart as if they'd been walking together by accident the whole time.

Emma started a page for herself in the boy book that night. Under her name she wrote: *Boy Hater?*

Chapter 14

After school the next day—the day after what might have been the worst in Emma's life—Emma tossed her books in her backpack and took off for Louise's house. Louise would be waiting for her there. She had stayed home sick that day.

It wouldn't be a big deal, normally, if some fifth-grader stayed home sick. People catch colds all the time, or at least pretend they have colds if there's some big math test or something. But Louise never stayed home. For one thing, she never got sick. She was immune to practically everything. When they were in the third grade and a flu epidemic had swept school, Louise was in charge of calling everyone to tell them what their homework was. Emma could even remember going on a picnic with Louise's family where she, Louise, and twenty of Louise's cousins went tromping through the woods. Louise was the only kid who didn't catch poison ivy.

The other thing was, Louise never faked being sick. It wasn't because of some strict moral code or anything. Louise had told Emma that if she stayed home and didn't look as if she was going to die, her mother would assign her some household task. No one stays home from school so they can clean out the basement.

Emma took the whole thing as a bad sign. Whether Louise was really sick or not, Emma felt she had somehow given up.

Louise opened the door, wearing a robe and sipping from a mug of chicken broth.

"You mean, you're actually . . ." said Emma.

Louise put her finger to her lips, then moved it away. "No. But if my mom figures it out, she'll make me wallpaper the bathroom or something. Let's go to my room."

Emma felt slightly relieved. At least faking showed a little spunk.

Louise climbed into her bed. "I just couldn't stand the idea of going in today."

"Just because Roger won't talk to you . . ." Emma started to say.

"It's not just that," Louise said. "I don't like everyone being so mad at us. I mean, it makes me think . . . maybe we're really doing something wrong."

"Wrong?" Emma was annoyed. "What could be wrong about science?"

"I don't mean the whole idea," Louise explained. "Maybe just parts of it. Maybe we're not being fair."

Emma felt a cold chill and shivered. Were they being unfair, like Aunt Marian had warned?

"Besides, we can't seem to prove anything for sure," Louise continued, talking quickly so Emma couldn't possibly interrupt, "so I think we should combine projects with the boys. I don't know if you can have four partners, but I bet we can tell the principal it'll be four times as much work as a normal project and . . ."

"You want to do our project with Roger and Wally?" asked Emma. She was too shocked to object. "And then just see who's right?"

Louise kept talking as if Emma hadn't spoken. "Once word gets out what's going on, we'll probably get the Nobel Peace Prize or something, with us all working together, boys and girls . . ."

"Louise!" Emma said. "Don't make up some crazy story for me. I *know* you, remember?"

Louise looked embarrassed. "I'm sorry. Sometimes I can't help it."

A loud knock came at the door, and Louise plunged deep under her covers. "Come in," she said in a weak voice.

Louise's mother stood in the doorway, wearing a plaid suit and white silk blouse. She worked as a legal secretary and always looked glamorous to Emma, like a secretary in a fancy TV office. She walked toward the bed, bestowing a passing smile on Emma.

"Honey, how do you feel?" Mrs. Zarotsky asked the lump in Louise's bed.

Louise slowly lowered the covers from her head. "I feel awful," she said. "I'm too sick to wash the dishes tonight."

"Well, of course you don't have to wash the dishes!" Louise's mom sounded genuinely surprised. "I'm worried about you, that's all. Just let me know if you need anything. I'll be in the kitchen."

As soon as Mrs. Zarotsky closed the door behind her, Louise sat up. "That was a close one," she said.

Emma was unconvinced. "She didn't look like she came in to order you around."

"You don't know her like I do," said Louise, dismissing her with a wave of her hand. "So, what about combining the projects? Wouldn't it be better to work with the boys? Then we'd know the results would be more, you know, unbiased."

"It makes sense," said Emma, warming to the idea. "No one can blame us when we prove girls are better than boys, if we can get boys to help us prove it."

"Exactly," said Louise. "Then the boys can't be mad at us anymore."

"O.K.," said Emma. "It'll be good for the project." She smiled at her friend. "And that's all you care about, of course. Not about what the boys think of you or anything."

Louise shrugged helplessly. Emma knew there was nothing Louise could say in her defense—she knew her friend too well.

A high-pitched shriek came from the kitchen. Emma jumped, but Louise didn't look at all alarmed. "A mouse," she said. "I must have caught another mouse in my trap." She threw off her bedcovers and went to the aid of her mother.

Chapter 15

It's pretty hard to convince someone who's not talking to you to talk to you about how he isn't talking to you. That is to say, there was no good way for Louise and Emma to approach Wally about their plan to combine projects with the boys. Emma staked out the cafeteria exit and started talking to Wally as soon as she saw him.

"Wally, I think you and Roger and Louise and I should all work on our project together," she said. "I mean, we're all doing the same thing, and it's just a waste of resources to have separate teams. It makes sense, don't you think?"

"Emma, I can't talk to you," said Wally, speeding down the hall. He didn't look back, as if he believed that if he didn't see her, she wouldn't be there.

But Emma matched his stride until there was only about an inch between Wally and the wall. "Wally, this is really important."

He didn't slow down. "You're going to get me in trouble."

"If you don't talk to me," said Emma, "I'm going to scream as loud as I can, and everyone's going to turn around and see us together."

Wally's eyes got wide. "Don't do that!" he said, and he opened the door to an empty classroom, gesturing for her to follow.

Emma sat down on top of a desk, and Wally stood in front of her. "Listen," said Emma. "Our project isn't . . . Well, I'm sure if we kept at it, we could prove what we need to, but time's running out, and . . . it just makes sense to work together."

"What?" asked Wally. He looked about as shocked as Emma had been when Louise had first proposed the idea. "You want us all to have one project?"

"Yeah," said Emma. "That way everyone will know we're being fair and everyone will talk to each other again." She hesitated before she told him any more. Could she really trust Wally? But she had to. "Louise feels really bad about how no one's talking to each other. And she really wants to talk to Roger again."

Wally smiled. "Roger wants to talk to Louise, too."

"He does?" asked Emma. "Wait'll I tell . . ."

Wally gave her a look that she immediately understood.

"I won't say anything," she told him. "So, listen, will you just find out from Roger if it's O.K.?"

Wally nodded. A return to nonverbal communication. Emma sighed.

They checked to see if anyone was in the hallway, then walked off in opposite directions so no one would know they'd been talking. By the next day, that sort of precaution would no longer be necessary.

There was no official announcement that the ban on talking to girls was lifted, but somehow everyone knew. Roger told his immediate circle, and by recess, the word had spread through all six grades. By lunch, Emma noted, conversations were happening between the sexes as if there had been no interruption at all.

Emma also noted—and she felt she was becoming more sensitive to this sort of thing—that there was still a lot of boy/girl tension. In the cafeteria she watched a third-grade boy get two desserts for lunch. A second-grade girl whispered to her friend, "See? No girl would ever do that."

In a similar incident, Emma witnessed a fifth-grade girl run and fall flat on her face in the playground. A group of sixth-grade boys laughed as she hit the pavement. One boy said, "I don't think there's a girl in this school that can outrun my six-year-old brother."

Emma realized that there had been fighting between boys and girls before they started their science project. But now both genders thought they had a right to be mean to the opposite sex, because they were so sure of their own superiority.

After school, when Emma, Louise, Wally, and Roger walked together across the schoolyard toward their first group meeting at Roger's house, the whole student body watched them go.

Chapter 16

Roger's basement had everything—an expensive stereo system, a wide-screen TV, and a couch big enough to sleep a family of twelve. But Emma was too nervous to enjoy the surroundings. She could tell Louise felt the same way. But neither of them could show it.

"So," said Emma, "what kind of evidence have you gathered so far?"

"Well," said Roger, clearing his throat, "we haven't exactly proved anything. But we did run some experiments. We definitely showed that boys make better paper airplanes. We also learned girls were better at penmanship."

Emma and Louise nodded at each other. Penmanship was one of the few subjects they could find any real difference on, too.

"But I guess that's about it," Roger admitted. "At least so far."

Wally nodded.

"O.K.," said Emma, "we got the penmanship thing, too. Plus we tried to find out who's more polite." Remember, thought Emma to herself, be scientific. "But I'm not sure that test was fair."

"So what we need, then," said Roger, "is some test that proves who's better for sure."

They were all silent for a minute.

"How about a race?" Roger asked. "They give out awards for racing all the time, so that shows it's important. We can have a bike race."

Emma knew that the Olympics had races, and the Olympics were really important. It seemed like a good suggestion to her.

"I don't think it means you're *better* just because you're *faster*," said Louise.

Emma was waiting for this statement to be accompanied by a long lie involving Louise and the International Olympic Committee, but that didn't happen. Louise just sat quietly.

"We can run other experiments later," Roger said. "Maybe you can think of the next one."

Emma noticed Roger was always extra polite when he spoke to Louise, but Louise only shrugged, barely looking at him. Emma felt slightly cheered. Maybe Louise was losing interest in Roger. Louise would be a lot better off when she stopped spending so much time thinking about him and spent more time thinking about science.

"I guess it's an O.K. idea for now," said Louise, "if you guys think so."

Everyone else seemed satisfied, so the planning for the first group experiment began.

Chapter 17

Emma called Louise after supper to check in. Someone picked up the phone, but all Emma heard was laughter—laughter that could only have come out of a slightly crooked mouth.

"Louise," said Emma, grinning herself, "what's so funny?"

"Oh, Emma." Louise sounded as if she'd been tickled continuously since breakfast. "Eddie's stuck in my trap. I put out a Hershey bar for the mice, and

he tried to swipe it. Now he's got a milk crate on his head!" Louise started laughing again.

"And he's supposed to be the smart one," said Emma, giggling.

"It's not just a mousetrap," said Louise, "it's a boy trap."

After she hung up the phone, Emma figured out something important. If Eddie had gotten caught in Louise's trap, he couldn't have known how it was made. And if he didn't know how it was made, he couldn't have helped Louise make it. She had done it all by herself.

That night Emma dreamed of Wally being trapped by a huge, boy-sized milk crate.

Emma swung back and forth on her favorite schoolyard swing and worried. She worried more effectively when she was swinging. She worried about her science project, she worried about Louise, and she worried that her hair would never grow back in.

As she swung higher, she spotted Wally on the playground. He didn't see her, so Emma swung wildly, trying to get his attention without seeming like she was trying to get his attention. It was no use. He kept staring off in the opposite direction.

That night Aunt Marian complained to Emma about her love life. "I tell you, Emma, I'm tired of going on dates. The next time I see a guy I like, I'm just going to go up and ask him, 'What are you doing for the rest of your life?' And if he doesn't have any plans, I'm going to convince him to hang out with me. I don't want to get married or anything. I'd just like some kind of semipermanent arrangement. I'm tired of all this breaking up and getting back together again. It's exhausting."

Conversations Aunt Marian and Emma had about men had been, up to this point, completely one-sided. In fact Emma had found them rather baffling. But now, for the first time ever, Emma had something to add.

"Aunt Marian," she began, "how do you get a boy to like you? If you don't know if he does or not?"

"Honey," said Aunt Marian, "if I knew that, I could earn a fortune and make millions of people happy. But if a boy doesn't like a girl, well, there's not much she can do."

This wasn't very good news to Emma. She opened her boy book to write in it, but nothing came to her.

Chapter 18

No one would ever know from the way Louise behaved that she had ever objected to the idea of a race. For a week in advance of the event, she trained heavily. She biked back and forth to school every day with a stopwatch around her neck to check her time. She did stretching exercises while in math class. Emma was pleased, not only because Louise was showing some enthusiasm, but because she figured there was a pretty good chance a girl would win the race.

Emma was also amused to note that Louise was engaged in psychological warfare against the competition. "I know I'm going to win because of this eye tic I have," she heard Louise say to Roger. "I always get eye tics when something really great is about to happen. I got one right before I won a $50 gift certificate to the mall and another one the time I got skipped a grade."

Emma couldn't help shaking her head at her friend, but she couldn't bring herself to contradict her, either. Louise had confided in Emma that she felt pretty weird about trying to make sure Roger liked her while simultaneously trying to beat him in a competition. Emma had told her that sometimes you have to sacrifice to find the truth.

The day of the race was beautiful. About a hundred kids, including Louise and Roger, lined up their bikes on Main Street, which was blocked off by traffic cones. The gym teacher, Ms. Standish, was going to blow the starting whistle, and Mrs. Marsh would judge the winners. Emma stood on the sidewalk with her clipboard. Since the race spanned only ten blocks, there probably wouldn't be time for notes, but Emma wanted to seem official. Wally merely stood next to her and folded his arms thoughtfully.

When Ms. Standish blew the whistle, it was about the loudest sound Emma had ever heard. Then a hundred bike-racing kids turned into a blur of a hundred bikes and two hundred arms and two hundred

legs and Louise gaining speed and Jeff cutting off
Linda and Linda yelling *eek* and accidentally swerving
into Toby and Toby slamming into the sidewalk and
Roger and Louise neck and neck and some third-
grade boy, his bike a whir of blue and gold, pedaling
like crazy and yelling *yahoo* and Jennifer getting her
shoelace caught in her front wheel . . .

Wally turned to Emma and said quietly, as if there
were nothing of any real interest going on, "Louise
was right. This doesn't prove anything."

. . . and Mrs. Marsh running toward the finish line
and stopping to help Toby up and yelling at Mark to
stop being so rude and Suzie chucking a rock at
Steven's front tire and a sixth-grade boy, Andrew,
coming up out of nowhere to pass Louise and Roger

and then Mrs. Marsh blowing the whistle to announce who won.

"Andrew Goldstein's the winner," said Mrs. Marsh, who seemed as breathless from the announcement as the entrants were from the actual race. "Louise Zarotsky is second."

Emma could hear some of the girls complaining that Mrs. Marsh was blind, and the contest wasn't fair because Andrew had some fancy European bike his parents bought him that practically went thirty miles an hour even when you didn't pedal. Emma thought the bike did seem fancy, and maybe the race wasn't fair. Besides, Andrew's legs were about as long as Louise's whole body. How could she possibly have beaten him?

Roger walked up to Wally and Emma, wiping the sweat off his forehead with his sleeve. "I guess that's one point for our side," he said.

"Sorry, Emma," said Louise, plopping herself on the sidewalk. She gave Roger a sweet smile. "But at least I beat Roger."

Roger smiled right back at Louise, even though Emma could tell he was trying not to.

"Congratulations on coming in second," Emma said. "There's no way you could have beat Andrew. Not with that million-dollar bike of his."

"The bike had nothing to do with it!" said Roger.

"Come off it, Roger," Wally put in, but he didn't say anything else.

Then there was only the sound of one first-grade girl, Karin, the last kid left on the street, crying because the chain had fallen off her bicycle.

Emma knew just how she felt.

Chapter 19

The day after the bike race, Emma experienced another shock to her system. She'd been swinging with all her books in her lap and, at a particularly high point, had lost her grip on her boy notebook. It flew off, and she didn't see where it landed. She had to find it before the bell rang. She called Louise over and begged her to scan the area by the kids' slide while Emma searched frantically around the swingset.

"What does it look like?" Louise asked. "Does it say anything on the cover?" She loyally shoved her arm through a patch of dense shrubbery for anything that felt like a notebook. "If we can't find it, we can always look after school."

"We have to find it now," insisted Emma, crawling around in the little kids' section. The notebook wasn't the sort of thing she wanted anyone else to read. If the wrong person found it, it wouldn't exactly help any boy/girl problems going on at the school.

When she didn't get an answer, Emma stood up and saw that Louise was sitting on a big rock.

Not only had she found the notebook—she had it open!

Emma ran over and grabbed it out of her hands. "Don't read that!"

Louise didn't even fight her—she'd obviously read enough. "How can you say you're being scientific?" she asked, shaking her head. "You're just doing this project because you want to prove you're better than boys—because you don't like them. How can you keep telling me there's nothing personal about our project when there is for you? You wrote right here that you're a boy hater!"

"But it has a question mark . . ." Emma trailed off weakly. It's hard to defend yourself when you're dead wrong.

"Emma, what if some boy had found this? No one would believe there was anything scientific about what we're doing."

"I know!" said Emma. "That's why I was so worried about finding it."

"You should be worried about why you wrote it in the first place. How do I know I can trust you to be fair on the project?"

"I'm really sorry, Louise." Emma's eyes burned, and she was close to tears. "I'll be better from now on, I promise."

"O.K., Emma. I'm counting on you."

When Emma's mother saw her at the end of the day, Mrs. Adams opened her arms to give Emma a good long hug. For the first time in years, Emma didn't try to resist.

"Honey, what's wrong?" asked Mrs. Adams. "It's not about the project you and Louise are working on, is it?"

Emma shook her head. It was too hard to explain, and she wasn't even sure she could if she tried.

Mrs. Adams brought Emma a glass of milk and a piece of cake, just like she had when Emma was in kindergarten. Emma drank her milk in one gulp.

"Louise's mother and I were talking, and I know Louise has been pretty moody lately, too," said Mrs. Adams. "I hope you girls know what you're doing."

Emma got rid of her boy book the next day, as soon as she got home from school. Just to be sure no one else would ever read it, she tore up every entry into little pieces and ground them up in the garbage disposal.

Chapter 20

●●●●●●●●●●●●●●●●●●●●●●●●●●●●●●●●●●●●●●●

"This doesn't prove anything," Roger was saying as he, Wally, Louise, and Emma bent over a photograph of the bicycle race. Someone had taken a picture just as Andrew crossed the finish line. Emma had trouble concentrating, because Wally's left arm was gently brushing her right arm. When Roger grabbed the photo, causing them to separate, Emma was embarrassed, though she couldn't say exactly why.

"It doesn't prove anything?" asked Louise. "It proves that five girls finished right after Andrew. Don't those five girls count for more than just one boy who barely came in first?"

In all the excitement of the race and the competition between Roger and Louise, no one had noticed that the Jennings twins, some girl in the sixth grade wearing a tiara, and Lulu, who had recently moved from Florida, all finished between Louise and Roger, who was seventh. Emma suspected the real reason Roger was being so grumpy was that it proved that he'd been beaten by five girls.

"Well, a boy still won, and that's what we said we'd go by," Roger answered.

For a minute Emma felt sorry for Roger. She could tell he wanted to be fair, but he just felt stubborn. It was like he wanted to make up for losing the race by winning this argument. Emma knew what it was like to want to be reasonable but not be able to do it.

"Well . . ." started Emma.

"We have to be sure we're being fair," said Wally. "If we're not going to be fair, why are we working together?"

That was precisely what Emma thought. The only reason she didn't immediately agree was that she was surprised those words had come out of Wally's mouth. Could this be a sign? Maybe she and Wally had telepathic powers. Emma was pretty sure her aunt Marian would like Wally.

"Yeah," said Emma, after a moment. "Wally's right."

"But we don't even know *how* to be fair," said Roger, looking miserable. "We're not sure how to prove anything! And the science fair is in two weeks!"

They all fell silent. Louise finally spoke. "I don't think you can prove who's better, boys or girls. If you could, we would have proved it already."

Wally nodded, and Emma found herself nodding along with him. Louise was right. And Emma was going to try extra hard to do what was fair from now on—she'd promised.

"It's true," said Emma. "But if we can't prove any-thing, then how can we win?" she groaned. "We'll never even get a decent grade!"

"Everyone at school will hate us," Roger pointed out. "They're counting on us to come up with an answer."

And then Roger stopped looking miserable. He looked less miserable than he'd ever looked before. Given the circumstances, Emma thought his expression made him seem slightly crazy, like some guy who's lost everything but smiles because he's convinced he's Santa Claus.

"You guys," said Roger, "no one but us knows we haven't proved anything yet."

"So what?" said Louise. "They'll all know in a few weeks. Who cares if they know now or then?"

"Well," said Roger, "we don't have to tell them."

"You mean we should lie?" Wally asked.

"Not exactly," said Roger. "We'll just . . . change the rules a little."

Change the rules? thought Emma. What does that mean?

"Me and Wally think boys are better than girls, and you two think the opposite. Just because we can't prove either way doesn't mean none of us are right. That's why I think we should just decide on a single test, and we'll all agree to go by that."

"You mean we'll just say boys are better than girls or girls are better than boys because of one test?" asked Emma. "Even if that test doesn't prove anything?" That didn't sound scientific at all.

"Maybe once we're in the ninth grade or something, we'll look back at our experiments and see that we really did prove one way or the other," said Roger. "But right now if we can come up with some definite answer, half the school will still like us, and we might still do O.K. at the science fair. If we don't decide, we're doomed."

"We do have to do something," said Louise. "I really need a good grade."

Emma knew that if Louise got a bad grade on the science fair, she'd probably fail science—it counted as a third of every kid's total grade, and Louise's other test scores hadn't exactly been good.

"O.K.," said Roger. "How about something like that paper-airplane contest?"

"No way," said Emma. "A boy would win that for sure. They make a lot more paper airplanes than girls do."

"How about the Young Inventors Contest?" suggested Louise. "If a girl wins that, we say girls are better. If a boy does, we say boys are better."

"The Young Inventors Contest?" asked Roger. "No one ever enters that. Not anyone with friends, anyway."

"They will if we tell them what's going on," said Emma. "We'll make everyone invent the same kind of thing, so it'll be a fair test."

"It has to be something that you can make in a lot of different ways," said Roger. Wally nodded approvingly.

Everyone was silent.

"How about mousetraps?" suggested Emma. "People are always making different kinds of mouse-traps."

Wally and Roger both agreed. Only Emma noticed Louise's suspicious expression.

"O.K.," said Roger, "we'll spread the word tomorrow."

I should have just done some stupid bread-mold project," said Louise to Emma later that afternoon. "Then Roger would still like me, the boys and the girls would be getting along, and I'd get promoted to sixth grade."

Louise was plowing through a pile of dirty dishes as she talked to Emma. Thanks to Mrs. Zarotsky, Emma had to share Louise's afternoon not only with a bunch of dirty dishes, but with some rugs that needed vacuuming, a cat that needed feeding, and a trip to the post office for stamps.

"Aw, come on, Louise," Emma said. "The girls are going to win. You've got a head start on everyone else. You've caught mice with your trap and everything." She picked at some dried tomato sauce on the kitchen table. "There's nothing to be nervous about."

"Sure there is." Louise swabbed the tomato sauce off with a damp sponge, then returned to the sink. "How can I win the Young Inventors Contest? I'm terrible in science. And even if I do win, what if the judges find out what we're doing? We'll probably all fail and get expelled."

"Louise!" Emma said. "We're not going to get expelled. We're not doing anything wrong. The important thing is to get the boys to admit that we're better than they are. And we *are* better, right? Why should we get expelled for telling the truth?"

"I thought the whole point of science was to prove things, not make things up," said Louise. "If we just wanted to get Wally and Roger to say girls are better than boys, why did we run all those tests? Why not just promise them candy bars for life or something? It seems like that would've been a lot easier."

"Louise," said Emma.

Louise cut her off before she could start. "What if I made my mousetrap all wrong? How am I supposed to know if it's any good?"

Mrs. Zarotsky breezed through the kitchen, kissing Louise on top of her head. "If you're talking about the mousetrap, I think it's very clever. I only wish every child were as helpful as you." Then she breezed out again.

As if on cue, Eddie stomped into the kitchen. He made a beeline for the refrigerator and didn't look at either Emma or Louise. He was almost always in his room reading, so he got very little sunlight. As a result, he was about the palest human being Emma had ever seen.

Emma saw his eyes flicker toward Louise. "If only I were a girl and knew how to wash dishes. Hey, do you have some time later to hand-wash my dirty underwear?"

Louise picked up a glass from the soapy water and turned around to face him. "Just because you're smart doesn't mean you're not a jerk," she said, making a motion with her arm that suggested she was

about to throw the glass at him as hard as she could. He bolted upstairs.

"C'mon Louise," said Emma. "Enter the Young Inventors Contest. Teach Eddie a lesson about what girls can do."

"O.K.," said Louise. "I'll do it. And if I don't win, it won't be my fault, because I'll try as hard as I can."

Chapter 21

"**A**unt Marian," Emma said into the phone in her parents' room. It was the most secluded room in the house. "It's me, Emma." Even though no one could see her, Emma's hand automatically went to check her bald spot, which was currently uncovered. It was growing in nicely, but she kept wearing the hat, partly because she liked how it looked.

"Oh, hi, Emma," Aunt Marian answered.

Emma thought she wasn't quite as happy to hear from her as usual. She felt a sudden wave of fear—could her aunt have found out about their deal to decide their science project? But how could she know? And why should Emma feel bad about the agreement? It was a little weird, but it wasn't really wrong, was it? Emma swallowed hard.

"I'm sorry, Emma. I'm a little out of it," Aunt Marian said. "I just found out something about a friend of mine that didn't make me very happy."

"Oh, yeah?" asked Emma. Was Aunt Marian talking about her? Didn't people always say stories were about some "friend" when they were really about you?

"I found out she cheated on her research," Aunt Marian said.

"Are you sure?" Emma suddenly became aware of how odd her voice was. It sounded terrible—

annoyingly high-pitched. Now that she really gave it a listen, she could hardly believe anyone would take anything she said seriously.

"Yeah, I'm sure," Aunt Marian replied. "And she did it just for her own ego—so she'd look good. She didn't even take into account that other people might base their work on her research. It could have had a real domino effect."

"Well," said Emma, feeling downright nervous, "maybe she meant well, and something just went wrong."

"Emma, you either do things honestly, or you're lying. It's not that complicated."

"Well . . ."

"Anyway, my roommate is the one who did it. Believe me, Liz knew what she was doing."

Emma leaned back on the bed and wiggled her toes. She felt a wave of happiness.

"Your roommate!" she said.

"Yeah, my roommate. I don't know why you sound so happy about it. It's not like this is a good thing."

"I'm not happy about it," said Emma, and as suddenly as it had come upon her, the wave of happiness passed. She felt like she was pressed down under the weight of some heavy object, kind of like the Wicked Witch of the East when the house fell on her.

"Liz was discovered, and now she's going to be thrown out of school. I don't know what she's going to do with that on her record."

Emma sat up again. "How will everyone know?"

"The scientific community's pretty small. Word gets around. If some kid in Illinois invented a fuel-efficient way of recycling plastic today, I'd probably know by noon tomorrow."

Noon tomorrow? Emma thought. Would the same thing apply to her science project? "Noon tomorrow?" she said, without even realizing it.

"Well, practically," said her aunt. "But, anyway, what about you, kid? How's that top-secret science project going?"

Emma felt a blush coming on. Sometimes talking on the phone was a lot easier than talking in person. "O.K., I guess."

"You don't sound very sure about it," said Aunt Marian.

"Well, I guess I'm not."

"You don't have to tell me about it if you don't want to. But I do know a little about science. I might be able to give you a little advice."

She already had given her some advice. Emma just didn't know if she was going to take it.

Chapter 22

●●

The only good thing about Louise's being so nervous on the day of the science fair was that keeping her out of trouble kept Emma's mind off how nervous she was herself.

"We conducted worldwide tests," Louise was telling one of the judges as she stood in front of the *Boys vs. Girls: Which Are Better?* poster. "Well, nationwide, anyway, to find out about how to present results at fairs like this one, and it turns out the delay factor works really well." Louise was tapping her left foot like mad. "That's why we've put out some evidence here, but we're waiting to announce what we found out until the end. . . ."

Sensing trouble, Emma tried to catch Louise's eye, then tilted her head to one side, ran her index finger down the side of her nose, and clapped her hands twice. Louise looked at her quizzically and came over.

"What are you doing?" she asked.

"I'm trying to stop you from getting us in trouble," Emma said. "Maybe you shouldn't talk unless you absolutely have to."

"It's kind of hard when people talk to me first," Louise said. "Especially judges."

Louise's mousetrap exhibit was covered with a white bedsheet in a booth next to the *Boys vs. Girls* area. Even Emma didn't know exactly what was under there. When Emma asked her about it, Louise just repeated her story about how delaying the results made presentations more effective.

"Louise, it's me!" Emma said, shaking her by the arm. "Why are you telling me this? I'm your best friend—I know you're just making it up."

Louise looked positively anguished. "I'm sorry. I just don't know what I'm saying anymore." She plopped down in a folding chair. "I'm just going to sit here and practice not saying anything." Then she closed her eyes and leaned back.

Louise was under twice the pressure Emma was. The science fair and the Young Inventors Contest were both held today. After the winner of the Young Inventors Contest was announced, their team would reveal the superior gender. They had two different posters designed, one for each outcome, and both were hidden under the project table.

Roger stood nearby, talking to one of the judges, Vice Principal Allen. Mr. Allen was the most serious person in the whole world, as far as Emma knew. There was no way to tell if he even liked you, because he never smiled.

"What exactly were your research methods, Roger?" asked Mr. Allen.

"Well," Roger answered, "we had lots of different methods, because it's such a complicated project. We tried to cover all different areas to be as fair as possible." It didn't sound like much of an answer, even to Emma.

"I see," said Mr. Allen, who advanced to the next exhibit on mummies and the ancient Egyptians.

"How's it going?" Emma asked Roger. She felt a little sorry for him, and since he was about to be proved inferior, there was no harm in being a little nice to him.

"Not that great," Roger said. He sat down next to Wally and put his elbows on their display table. It contained mostly charts and graphs comparing boys' and girls' grades, ability to make paper airplanes, politeness, etc. All of which, Emma knew, proved nothing.

"Who do *you* think's going to win?" she asked him, curious to see what he'd say.

Out of the corner of her eye, she saw Mr. Allen jerk his head around from the mummy display and stare at her.

She continued in a loud voice, "I mean, win the Young Inventors Contest. Not who's going to win our project, because, of course, I already know that." Roger gave her a look that confirmed she sounded as crazy as she thought she did. "And not like one has anything to do with . . ."

Emma felt herself trip on something. She lost her balance and fell back onto something soft—Wally's coat. He held up the rope he'd tripped her with.

"Thanks, Wally," she said.

Wally nodded and gave her a thumbs-up. He helped her stand, and Emma became painfully aware of how sweaty her palms were. She felt gross and fishy.

When she turned around, both Roger and Mr. Allen were giving her the evil eye.

Then Emma saw something that made her completely forget how horrible she felt at that moment. Because she knew, in a very short time, her situation was about to become much worse.

Chapter 23

●●

Two women walked through the door of the auditorium—Louise's mother and Emma's aunt Marian. What could those two possibly be doing here? wondered Emma. They weren't together. Neither had said anything about showing up. Aunt Marian was supposed to be at school. And Mrs. Zarotsky only made appearances when Eddie had some big event. Of course, Louise had probably never had a big event before.

Could they have discovered the plan? Would they expose the science project as a fraud?

Aunt Marian spotted Emma and gave her a wave and a big smile. Emma felt a little better. That wasn't the behavior of someone out to ruin her academic career.

"Emma, that hat looks great on you," said Aunt Marian. Emma touched the green felt fondly. "So is this the winning booth, or what?"

"Why aren't you in school?" Emma asked.

"It's vacation. And I wanted to be here for your big day, especially since you've been keeping your project such a secret. Aren't you happy to see me?"

"Yeah," said Emma, and she meant it. No matter how bad things were, she was always happy to see Marian.

Aunt Marian read their poster, and Emma thought she heard her giggle, but she couldn't be sure. "Your mom's coming a little later." Marian raised her eyebrows. "I'm sure she won't be disappointed."

Louise's mother also found the booth.

"Mom," said Louise, "Eddie's grade has its science fair separately. Today's is just for the elementary school."

"Emma's mother called and reminded me that today's your big day. I wanted to see what's been keeping you so busy lately. I'm happy to see both my children's events, as long as they tell me when they are."

But then they were cut off by Mr. Allen speaking into a microphone. "Welcome, everyone. Inventors, please go to your tables. Judging will begin in a moment."

All the young inventors ran to their inventions while the group of judges gathered, led by Mr. Allen. Mrs. Zarotsky joined the audience. "Welcome to the Kennedy Elementary School Young Inventors Contest, everyone," said Mr. Allen. He walked over to Jason Weiner's invention. "Now, this first project is a mousetrap, right, Jason?"

"It sure is," Jason said.

"And what is it that makes your mousetrap so special?"

"Um . . ." Jason said, as an intro to absolutely nothing else. Then he started again. "It's . . . I made it out of stuff from my garage."

What else could he say? thought Emma. Jason had constructed the most generic mousetrap possible. When you hear the word mousetrap, Jason's contraption is what you picture.

Mr. Allen and the judges walked to the next table. "Moira O'Keeffe, what do we have here?" he asked.

"It's a trap," said Moira, "for mice."

"I see," said Mr. Allen. "How very original. And how does it work?"

Moira demonstrated. "You see, the mouse sees its reflection in the mirror here." She pointed to the back of the trap. "Then, when it hits this rubber band, the sliding door shuts. Then this little bell rings," Moira said, indicating a tiny bell on top. She rang it to make sure he understood. "See?"

"I see," said Mr. Allen. "And what makes this mousetrap especially effective?"

"Well . . ." said Moira.

"Is it more efficient than other traps? Does it work better on certain types of mice? At certain altitudes?"

"I'm not sure about that," whispered Moira.

"Well, why did you make it? There must be some reason you wanted to invent a better mousetrap instead of a better bicycle or a better eggbeater." Mr. Allen waited. Emma stuck her thumbnail into her arm really hard to keep from screaming. Be strong, Moira! Emma thought. Don't tell him!

"Um . . ." said Moira as the whole room watched. "I don't know why."

Emma removed her thumbnail from her arm as the judges made their way down to the next inventor. She glanced at Wally's arm and noticed a series of thumb marks. She felt a pang of solidarity.

"He knows something's going on," Wally whispered. Mr. Allen stood stonefaced before another mousetrap project.

"How could he know?"

Wally shrugged and made a sweeping gesture with his hand, covering the entire room.

Emma shook her head. "No kid would tell him anything about it. That would be such a loser thing to do."

Even as she made this proclamation, essentially vouching for the character of every kid at Kennedy Elementary, she knew she didn't mean it. How could she possibly trust all six hundred kids? Especially when half of them were boys and therefore impossible to trust? She scanned the room for traitors. If anyone had ratted them out, it was obviously a boy.

"Even if Mr. Allen thinks there's something strange about all the mousetraps," Emma told Wally, "he doesn't really know what's going on."

Roger joined them. "There she goes," he said as Mr. Allen faced Louise and her project. "I hope he isn't too mean to her."

Roger seems more nervous than Louise does herself, Emma thought. But he still doesn't want her to win. Just because he's being nice doesn't mean he wants a girl to win any more than any other boy in the room does.

Mr. Allen stopped in front of Louise's table. Louise winked at Emma as she yanked the bedsheet off her project with one swift motion.

Underneath was a collection of very large traps. They were a lot like the first one Louise had made but bigger. Emma wondered if they were designed to catch mutant mice after some freak nuclear accident.

Mr. Allen sneered slightly. "Let me guess, are these mousetraps?"

Louise smiled widely, the same smile that she'd used when she had tried to convince Mr. Ergemeyer to let her out of detention because she had the Ebola virus. "No, Mr. Allen," she said. "I did a lot of research on mousetraps, and plenty of great mousetraps have already been thought of. If you even study the hieroglyphics of the ancient Egyptians . . ."

Emma made a zip-lipping gesture to Louise and cut short what could have been a whopper lie.

"So I decided I'd make another kind of trap. A boy trap."

Emma noticed her aunt Marian giggling, and it seemed unusually loud. Then she realized the whole room was filled with giggling. A boy trap? Emma was too surprised to laugh. Why hadn't Louise told her?

Mr. Allen, who was probably not used to so much silliness at a Young Inventors Contest, didn't know what to do. He seemed at a loss for a follow-up question. Another judge spoke up. "A boy trap?" she asked. "But why would you want to trap boys?"

At this point the laughing got louder, and Louise dropped her getting-out-of-detention smile for her standard slightly crooked grin. "There are only two reasons to catch boys," she said. Then Emma saw Louise turn to face Roger as though she were answering his question and not the judge's. "Either because you like them or because you don't like them."

At that, the whole room broke into laughter. Roger simply looked thoughtful. Emma figured he was probably trying to figure out which category he fit in.

Louise went on to demonstrate exactly how the traps worked, and the different kinds of bait: candy bars, comic books, and video games. Even though Mr. Allen and the others kept asking questions, it was pretty obvious who was that year's Young Inventors winner.

My best friend is really smart, Emma realized, and she was proud of her. How could she not have noticed how smart Louise was before?

Aunt Marian leaned over to Emma during the commotion and whispered, "I guess Louise has got this contest all wrapped up. But who do you suppose is going to win the science fair?" She winked at Emma.

Emma smiled widely. Aunt Marian would think that smile meant Emma felt confident that their project would win the fair. But Emma smiled because something much more important had just happened—girls had just been proved better than boys.

"What do you mean it doesn't count?" Emma whispered to Roger as they stood side by side at the front of the *Boys vs. Girls* booth. Louise had just been announced as the winner of the Young Inventors Contest, and Emma had given Wally the signal to put up the *Boys vs. Girls: Girls Proved Better* poster.

"Some kids are saying that the contest isn't fair because Louise didn't make a mousetrap," said Roger. Emma could tell exactly which kids, since there was a crowd of boys and girls gathering in front of the booth, gesturing and talking to each other. Emma wondered if this was what was meant by an angry mob. She felt a wave of panic.

"Keep it down, you guys," Roger said, taking the words right out of Emma's mouth. All the action was starting to attract the attention of the judges. Louise stepped off the stage, clutching her award, and her mother gave her a big hug.

Aunt Marian had worked her way through the crowd of kids to see what was happening. The kids cleared a path, probably thinking she was one of the judges. In a way, Emma thought, she was the most important judge. "Is everything O.K., Emma?"

Mrs. Adams showed up at that moment, and Emma covered her face with her hands. "Emma," she said, looking at the commotion. "You're not causing trouble, are you?"

"This is terrible," said Emma, her panic becoming despair. Mr. Allen headed toward the booth at a brisk pace. She knelt beside Wally and the posters, then tore off only the *Boys vs. Girls* part of the one they were going to put up. She wrote *Neither Are Better* beneath it, and Wally helped her, just as if there had been no change in plan. They taped the poster up and turned around to see Mr. Allen reading it.

His arms crossed and his lips pursed, Mr. Allen looked like he did every other day in the history of the world—stern and unhappy. Louise ran up behind him. She took one look at the poster, opened her mouth, then shut it again.

"What's the purpose of this project?" Mr. Allen asked.

Louise stepped in front of him and stood with her shoulder solid against Emma's. "We just wanted to show whether boys or girls are better."

"So we did all these tests," Roger threw in, "to show who's faster and who can make better paper airplanes . . ."

"And who's more polite," said Emma. She blushed a little when she realized she wasn't exactly proving how polite girls were by interrupting Roger.

"And what have you concluded?" asked Mr. Allen, as he pored through the documents and diagrams at their table.

"We didn't prove anything," Roger said.

Wally stood up. "Yes, we did," he said.

Emma was pretty surprised to hear Wally say anything, especially at such a high-pressure moment. But she was glad to hear him talk.

"We proved that you can't prove which are better, boys or girls, because neither are better," Wally said. "And we proved that it's probably not a good idea to try to prove anything like that, anyway."

Mr. Allen crossed and then recrossed his arms. "I see," he said. "So you've proved nothing, then."

They were going to fail, Emma realized. She was going to receive a failing grade for the first time ever. She'd never gotten anything below a B+ in anything besides gym.

Emma couldn't think of a word to say to defend their project. Fortunately, Louise was on the case. "Proving something *isn't* true is as valuable as proving something *is* true," she said.

Mr. Allen unpursed his lips and formed them into a half smile. It looked surprisingly natural. "That makes sense, I suppose," he said. He made some notes on his clipboard and moved on to the next booth.

Emma was amazed—Louise had charmed Mr. Allen. Once you win an inventors' contest, people start thinking of you in a whole new way—even Mr. Allen.

"I wish Eddie could see this," Mrs. Zarotsky said to Louise. "He'd be so proud of you."

Louise rolled her eyes at Emma. "Well, Ma, in a way he inspired me, you know?" she said to her mom. "He helped me get the idea for the boy trap, even though he didn't do it on purpose."

"It's so great to see you kids helping each other," Mrs. Zarotsky said. Sometimes mothers just didn't get sarcasm, Emma noticed.

Roger cleared his throat. "Congratulations on winning the contest, Louise." He extended his hand. "I always knew you were really smart."

"Nobody else did," she said, shaking his hand. "Including me."

Emma helped Wally tear up their unused posters. "I guess none of this would've happened if you'd just been my science partner in the first place."

Wally smiled a mischievous smile. "I've got an idea for next year's project."

Emma was scared to ask the question, but she forced herself. "Next year we're definitely going to be partners, right?"

"Yeah," said Wally. "I promise." And they shook on it.

Chapter 24

"**L**isten to this," said Louise. Emma concentrated on the other end of the phone line. She heard some clinking and splashing.

"What is it?" Emma asked.

"It's the sound of Eddie doing the dishes!" said Louise. Emma thought she heard a grumble from Eddie. "My mom really gets it now. She even asked me if I want to be an inventor when I grow up."

"Wow," said Emma. "Everything's worked out pretty well. No one at school seems too mad that we didn't prove anything."

"I heard a bunch of girls talking in the bathroom about us," said Louise. "They said a lot of kids are just happy they got extra credit for their inventions. I heard the judges saying this year had the most entries for the Young Inventors Contest ever."

"Well," said Emma, "at least we know they got the most mousetrap entries ever."

"Definitely," said Louise.

"I hope our B- doesn't bring down my term grade too much," Emma said.

"We were lucky to get that," said Louise, "after everything that happened. Do you think anyone ever figured out what we were up to?"

"Not exactly," said Emma. "I think they just knew we were up to something."

Emma felt her aunt Marian tap her on the shoulder; she was staying at their house for a few days while her college was on break. "You have a visitor," she said.

"A visitor, huh?" asked Louise, overhearing. "Anyone I know?"

Emma could see Wally's figure through the screen door. "I have to go," she told Louise. "I'll call you later."

"Well, good, because I want to hear all about what happens with Wally."

There's no point in trying to hide anything from your best friend, Emma realized. She'd just figure it out, anyway—especially a smart friend like Louise.

Aunt Marian tugged Emma's hat off her head.

"Aunt Marian!" cried Emma. "What are you doing?" Wally could see perfectly well from where he was standing, and she wasn't going to have him come in while she was walking around with her bald spot perfectly visible. "I need my hat!"

"Oh, Emma," her aunt replied, "your hair is all grown in. Haven't you noticed?"

Emma felt her head and realized she couldn't even tell where the gum

O•k

107

had been. How could that have happened without her knowing? It was getting pretty hard to keep tabs on anything, with everything happening so fast.

"I hoped you'd like this hat," Aunt Marian said, "but you shouldn't wear it all the time. You have such beautiful hair."

Emma stroked her hair with her right hand and felt how soft it was. She did have nice hair. It was her best feature.

She walked over to open the door to let Wally in. "I guess you must have figured out I don't hate you," said Emma.

"Well, you can't, now," said Wally as though he'd spoken in complete sentences his whole life, "because we've proved I'm just as good as you are."

Emma cleared her throat. "Hey, Wally, what are you doing for the rest of your . . . I mean, the rest of the afternoon? Maybe we can think of some ideas for next year's science fair."

They drank lemonade and brainstormed topics for hours, avoiding anything controversial. Wally came up with some good ideas, Emma thought. If anyone had asked, she would have had to admit he was as smart as any girl.